Skeleton Crew

ALLAN AHLBERG · ANDRÉ AMSTUTZ

GREENWILLOW BOOKS, NEW YORK

Produced by Mandarin; printed and bound in Hong Kong   First American Edition   10 9 8 7 6 5 4 3 2 1

Library of Congress Cataloging-in-Publication Data
Ahlberg, Allan.
  Skeleton crew / by Allan Ahlberg ;
pictures by André Amstutz.
      p.   cm.
  Summary: Three skeletons have a good time
on their sailing vacation, until their
boat is boarded by pirates.
  ISBN 0-688-11436-9 (trade)
  [1. Skeleton—Fiction.   2. Sea stories.
3. Vacations—Fiction.   4. Humorous stories.]
I. Amstutz, André, ill.   II. Title.
PZ7.A2688Sk   1992   [E]—dc20
91-39161   CIP   AC

The big skeleton catches a little fish
and throws it back.
He catches a big fish and keeps it.
He catches a bigger fish . . .

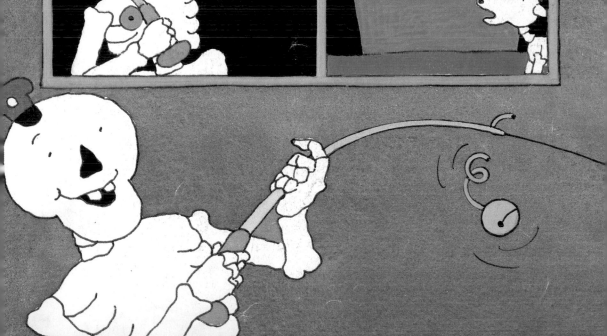

And – "Yo – ho – ho!" –
the pirates come.

The pirates climb aboard
looking for treasure.
They steal the deck chair
and the hammock.

nothing happens.

But the <u>next</u> night,
under a starry sky
and over the deep blue sea,
the skeletons spy . . . a tree.
"Yippee!"

On the island
the big skeleton
finds a parrot.
"Pretty Polly!"

The next night a lot happens.
A storm blows up.
The thunder crashes,
the lightning flashes,
the wind howls
and the dog howls, too.
"Howl!"

As quick as a blink
the raft is blown
across the foam . . .

The End (or is it?)

The End